CM00871777

Γ

IN

DISGUISE

WRITTEN BY

SARAH MOHAMED

FRONT COVER ILLUSTRATED BY

NAYYIRAH ABDULLAH

TO MY MOM, DAD

AND MIEKE

- Chapter One -

My Day

It was an ordinary day at Canfield Primary. Well ordinary for everyone except for Flora McGonall.

Flora was a twelve year old deaf student, who seemed to have a mind like Albert Einstein. Although Flora was a smart student, she was always known for being the biggest bully target. Flora was bullied for being deaf. As she walked around, people would want to stay as far as possible from her.

Flora was deaf, but that didn't stop her from doing the normal kind of things that kids did.

Flora kept a diary. She'd write in it every day, without fail. The only friends that she really had was her little husky, her parents and her diary.

Flora got her husky for her 12th birthday, she named her Loki. Flora had an elder sibling who had passed away in a car crash. She never really spoke about her. Her sister's name was Loki, so she named her puppy Loki, after her late sister. Flora's parents were kind and they were a wealthy family.

Flora would enter school, shaking in trepidation, but she wouldn't show her fear. Because Flora was deaf, Flora could understand and interpret people's mouthing and lip movements from one to another. Her nickname was Fifi.

Flora's cousin, who went by the name of violet, also went to the same school as Flora. Flora *hated* her. Every time Flora saw her, Flora's eyes would fill with flames and fury.

It was because of her, Flora's nickname was publicised to the whole school.

Violet was unusually spoiled for an average twelve year old and was admired by many of her family members. Her father, who was Flora's uncle from her mother's side, had not known about this. Flora though it was time to burst her cousins play time.

She wrote a note that read,

Dear Uncle Thomas,

I think it's time you know the truth. Violet has been a pain in my arm. She has been pushing me, making fun of me, making me do her homework, and when I do her homework, she'll rip mine up... I was hoping to speak to you about this and I finally think now is the time...

From your niece,

Flora.

The bullies would come and pick on Flora. They'd take her lunch and steal her drawings.

Flora was a good writer, but she was a better artist. She would come home, write in her diary and then set off to draw all the things that she would feel in her heart. Drawing also helped Flora, as she could draw her emotions rather that speaking it.

TTTRRRRIIIING!

'Finally! The end of the day!' Flora thought, feeling relieved. Flora waited for her mum to pick her up from school, so she could go and enjoy the rest of her day in her villa. Flora thought that today she'd go home, write in her diary and then do some drawing and jump in the pool.

Flora's mum picked her up from school and went home. Flora ate a snack and ran off to her room to write in her diary.

In her mind, she thought, 'Ahhh, time to relax and write in my diary.'

"Dear Diary," it read.

Today was no different to the others, we had Maths, English, Chemistry, physics, Library, Arabic and Art. Today Sophie and the other mean girls came up to me and just started calling me names. They didn't know that I was wearing my hearing aid. What they said about me hurts, just when I think of it. They called me an ugly mindless alien. Am I really a mindless alien?

Oh, if I were just a normal girl, even for one day. I'd appreciate it. I wish I had friends, I mean, if I was normal, I'd have friends. Loki makes me think of my sister. I mean I named her Loki. Its the only name that makes me happy. Eh, either way, she's gone from this world....

Flora looked down at the floor and tears started to form in her eyes. Flora knew she should stay strong. She knew her sister was now in a better place.

Flora changed into a swimsuit and headed to the pool. Loki was outside, near the pool waiting for Flora to come. Flora ran and jumped into the pool with a big splash.

Loki put her paw into the water and took it out. She was scared of the ice cold water. Flora was having the best time of her life.

Soon, her parents came and decided to hop in too. Floras mum was getting a tan while Floras dad joined Flora in the pool. He started to shiver because he was cold.

Three hours later..

Flora, in sign language said to her dad, "Look! my fingers are old!" He chuckled and gave Flora a hug.

Flora got out of the pool, took a warm bath and jumped into her pyjamas. She came out of her room and then went to the dining hall with a pencil, notebook and an eraser. She started to draw a picture of a realistic girl with the solar system around her head.

Flora took a picture and posted it on Instagram. She ate dinner, enjoying rice and chicken. She then drank a glass of apple juice.

Flora then went to bed. Overnight, her phone started to blast with notifications. She didn't wake up as she was in a deep, deep, DEEP sleep.

- Chapter Two -

The House Celeb

The next morning Flora got up, stretched out her arms and reached out for her phone. Flora checked her notifications and dropped her phone on her bed. It felt like a dream. She couldn't believe it. Her drawing had gone viral.

Flora got a DM from the Instagram owners asking her if she'd wanted to be verified. She immediately replied with a huge smile on her face.

In a few hours, Flora became a rising celebrity on the internet. She originally started with 91 followers, and now she had reached over 40,000. Eventually, Flora's parents later found out about their daughter's success on becoming one of the best artists, having her creative pieces shown around the world.

Flora was excited and thought that she could make a living out of being an artist. Her hopes were high, sky high.

Flora got ready for her day. She was pumped up with joy. She drew something and posted it on her account. The post got 24,000 likes in no time. Flora had earned $50 from her latest post and to her, it felt like a dream come true.

Each day her account grew larger and larger. By the end of the week, Flora had earned almost $300. For the weekend, Flora's parents decided to visitor Zanzibar (in Tanzania) for a week to congratulate her. She packed all of her essentials and they headed to the airport. Packs of people formed a crowd around Flora, where all of them were waiting for a picture.

Flora was overwhelmed with excitement. She wanted to take pictures with every single one of her fans, although her flight was waiting and of course, she couldn't miss her flight. She apologised to a few fans and ran to her plane, not wanting to delay it any further.

After a long 12-hour flight, Flora and her family had arrived in paradise.

There were fresh green trees scattered carefully and beautifully around the entire place, light blue lagoons privately nestled amongst the overgrown native trees, and amazing people welcoming Flora and her family with open hearts. A bus came to pick up Flora and her family, to take them to the resort.

"Welcome to Zanzibar, a paradise on earth!" one of the locals called, as they walked through the stunning resort. Flora was amazed.

The roses made a path, leading to the path to the reception. Flora sat on a chair, waiting, while her parents checked them in. She sat there on a chair that made her feel that she was sinking inside it. Flora took her sketchbook and pencil from out of her bag and started to draw. She started to draw some fish flying around the Eiffel Tower.

Suddenly, the fish that she drew jumped out of her book. She made the loudest gasp that she'd ever done. *GASP*

Flora's Mum turned around like lightning towards Flora. Floras' mum's eyes enlarged on the spot. There was a yellow fish here, a blue fish there and a green fish above her dads head.

Flora didn't know what had happened. It happened all so suddenly.

Flora closed her sketchbook. The fish disappeared into thin air! Flora's mind was popping with curiosity but Flora's mum was panicking. No one had ever seen this kind of magical moment ever before.

Flora's parents finished booking into the hotel and went to their room, eager to talk about what had happened with Flora's sketchbook and the fish.

"What was that back there? One minute the area is tranquil and clear, the next minute, fish are taking over the lobby," Flora's Mum said in a straight forward voice.

"I- I- I don't know!" Flora said in sign language.

"What do you mean you don't know?" Flora's mum questioned.

"I mean I don't know, by I don't know!" Flora replied.

Flora's mum let out a sigh. "When... when did this start?" Floras mum asked while stuttering.

"Just now! Even you saw it happen for the first time!" Flora said in an annoyed tone.

"Calm down both of you!" Flora's dad shouted.

Flora and her mum turned their heads to face Flora's dad. Flora's mum took a deep breath in and then slowly let it out, hoping to calm down.

Flora didn't need to hear her dad scream for her to know that he was upset.

- Chapter Three -

The Grip

After the argument, Flora took her sketchbook out of her bag and started to draw. Flora drew a Centaur with wings, wondering if the same phenomena would happen again. It did!

Once again, her sketch came to life. The mythical creature came to life and took flight right from out of her sketchbook. Flora pointed her pencil towards the bathroom and the Centaur flew towards the bathroom. With a sharp movement, she flicked her pencil up. Again, the centaur followed the pencil.

It was amazing. Flora had so many mixed emotions. She was excited, anxious, confused and amazed, all at once. Flora dramatically closed the sketchbook. In the blink of an eye, the Centaur was gone.

'WOW!' Flora thought to herself.

She wondered, 'Is this something a normal human can do? Am I finally a normal person?'

Flora decided that it was enough drawing for one day and enough surprises also for one day.

Flora placed her sketchbook upon the table and went off looking for her parents. Her parents were outside waiting for Flora to come, so they all could go to dinner.

Flora went to dinner and ordered a small burger and a soft drink. After dinner, when Flora and her family left the restaurant, they were welcomed with a pitch black path as they walked. Flora took one step and a path of torches automatically turned on. The torches led all the way to her room. Her eyes widened in amazement and her jaw dropped. She rubbed her eyes. Was she dreaming?

Flora returned back to her hotel room, which was warm by now. She kicked her shoes off and jumped onto the bed. It was one whole tiring day for Flora.

- Chapter Four -

The Bubble

After a long and full nights rest, Flora checked her phone to suddenly find a text message from the girls who used to bully her at school.

The message read:

From Sophie: at 9:00 PM.

I FOUND THE MINDLESS ALIEN IN MY CONTACTS? OH WHAT A SURPRISE! ANYWAYS, DON'T THINK THAT JUST BECAUSE YOU'RE A HUGE CELEBRITY THAT ANYTHING WILL CHANGE BETWEEN US. IT'S NOT LIKE YOU WILL GET ANY ATTENTION FOR ANYTHING, DOUBT IF YOU EVEN DREW THAT. I KNOW YOU USED A PRINTER FOR IT. I WILL MAKE SURE THAT YOU WILL GO DOWN, AND NOT UP...

'Wow... what shall I do? Do I tell mum? Or dad? Or anyone?!' Flora thought to her self.

Flora kept her phone down and just stared up at a blank white wall, wondering what on earth sparked such a rude and hurtful message. Her mind set on wondering if she should tell anyone, or just reply to Sophie. She couldn't decide. She was over thinking it so much that her fast was beating fast, so fast that it felt like her heart was running a mile per second.

Flora's mum came in with room service breakfast. Flora ate breakfast in her bed. She felt like she was receiving first class service.

"Make sure to get ready soon Flora, we are heading out today for our trip. We are having a beautiful picnic on an island," Flora's mum informed Flora.

After enjoying their breakfast, Flora and her family got ready for their day and waited outside, under the hot beaming sun, for the buggy to collect them and take them to the boat. After a twenty five minute wait, the buggy finally arrived.

A man approached them and said, "Sorry ma'am, your trip has been cancelled, as an unusual force of sorts has come and covered the resort from the north to the south."

"I'm sorry, but what?" Flora's dad gasped.

"I said an unusual force has taken over the resort," he repeated.

"Umm... I guess if there is an issue I can't force you to fix it," Flora's mum responded strangely.

- Chapter Five -

The Dark Force

Flora walked up to her mum and tapped her on the shoulder. "Mum, did the buggy driver say that black smoke was covering the island?"

"What do you mean Black smoke?"

"There's black smoke above the resort," Flora's mum peeked her clueless head out the window to find black smoke covering the resort. A notification ping on Flora's phone appeared.

From: Sophie at 11:37 AM

LOOK WHO I FOUND IN MY CONTACTS AGAIN! THE IDIOT, WHO THINKS SHE'S A REAL ARTIST. ANYWAYS STAY AWAY FROM BLACK, COULD HURT YOU REAL BAD. HEH...

"Stay away from black, Stay away from black? Stay away from black! She's behind all this... this.. this CHAOS!" Flora had solved the puzzle.

"The unknown bubble... and the smoke... It's all HER. MUM! DAD! STAY AWAY FROM THE BLACK SMOKE! I KNOW WHY IT'S HERE!" Flora, in sign language gestured.

"Why?" Flora's mum and dad asked in unison.

"One of the bullies from school. Sophie to be exact! She messaged me and said that she'll do ANYTHING to bring my fame and reputation down. She sent me a message ten minutes ago saying to stay away from black."

"What's that got to do with her?" Flora's dad said and then continued. "How did SHE know about the smoke, the bubble, the chaos?"

"Oh... uhm..." Flora's dad became nervous. "I- I see your point dear..."

"Sorry Mum and dad, I've got to do something." At once, Flora took out her notebook and her pencil. Flora walked out of her room and drew a horse with wings and a saddle.

She climbed on the creature that she had just drawn. The horse took off into the gloomy sky. A deep voice called out, "Flora...Flora McAdams."

Black smoke had been part of the reason she was deaf. When Flora was small, she had been caught in a fire. Black smoke had engulfed and entered her ear, and caused a major problem inside her brain, which in turn caused Flora to become deaf.

A shaped in human form walked towards Flora and the majestic horse. "Here, take this gift from me, or shall I say, my pen pal. Perhaps you know her? Her name begins with 'S'". Now things were getting just too strange.

'Who were these people and how did Sarah have so much power?' Flora wondered.

A small black cloud flew directly towards Flora and it engulfed her. She gasped a sound and suddenly realised something, "What?" she stopped. "Did... did... did you just give me a voice?"

The man in the cloud chuckled, "Not me, but..." the deep voice paused.

"Actually, guess who gave you your gift, remember her name starts with an 'S'..."

"S?" Flora repeated.

The only person she could think of was... "Sophie!"

"Well, well, well, that was a fun game of guess who, wasn't it?" The human form sarcastically said.

Flora took out her pencil and sketchbook. She drew a diamond sword with lightning power. The sword appeared in her hand. She looked up at the figure then back down to her parents.

Her mum nodded with tears in her eyes. "Since you've given me a voice, I can do this... CHARGE!!!" She screamed out.

The horse took off and aimed directly for the man. While upon the horse's back, Flora drew a box around the man, locking him in. When she was sure that it had taken effect in reality, she approached him.

"TAKE AWAY THIS BUBBLE NOW!" Flora said with rage and fury in her eyes.

"Not until you take the box away!" he demanded.

Flora knew and suspected his tricks, so she drew another box covering the first box, and erased the first box. Then she controlled the box to move from side to side, and at full speed, she threw the box out of the bubble. The black, gloomy sky turned back to its original light blue, shimmering sky.

'WHO was this man? His background?' Thought Flora. 'And what is the story behind him?'

- Chapter Six -

The Reward

the day of the flight to America

"Oh, how sad it is to go back to America," Flora's Mum said, when it was time for them to leave their amazing but strange holiday.

"Tell me about it!" Flora's dad added.

"Wait! Wait!" A man called from behind the family.

"Yes? Who are you?" Flora's dad said.

"I am the President of Tanzania, I have come to reward Flora McAdams with a small gift."

"Flora! Come here!" Flora's mom instructed.

"Yes?"

"Are you Flora McAdams?" The man enquired.

"Yes, yes I am," Flora answered.

"Thank you, for not only saving the guests in the resort, but the people of Tanzania."

"Oh, no problem!"

"I would like to reward you with something." He reached into his pocket and took a medal out. "Here, please have this. It is a gift to you, from me and my people."

Flora politely took the beautiful medallion and and said, "Thank you!"

"Wait! Before you go, I would like to say..." he paused.

"Say what?"

"Say... that..."

"Uhm, Flora, Our flight is in a few minutes..." Mum said, in a worried tone.

"Wait! He's trying to say something," Flora bursted.

The president smirked. "NOW!" He shouted.

Suddenly, upon his order, a metal cage flew around Flora and her parents and blocked them, locking them inside.

The president unzipped his what became clear, his professionally made prosthetics suit, and out walked what appeared to be a young girl. She didn't reveal her face at all.

"Don't think the war is over yet..." she announced.

About the Author

Sarah Mohamed

Sarah is a fabulously imaginative ten-year old writer based in Dubai. She enjoys writing short stories.

Sarah's favourite subjects at school are English, PE and Music. She loves to swim and cook, and she is also a huge football fan.

Amongst many of her achievements, Sarah won 1st place in the heat of the Hamdan Swimming Competition in Dubai recently. When she leaves school, she may become a professional swimmer.

To make the world a better place, Sarah would raise awareness of the true importance of our planet's well-being through creating a safer and cleaner place.

Printed in Great Britain
by Amazon